THE CELL of the GODS

THE CELL *of the* GODS

HOWARD J. BASTIAN

The Cell of the Gods

Paperback ISBN: 978-1-952062-66-7
Ebook ISBN: 978-1-952062-67-4

Published by Howard J. Bastian   06/04/2021

CONTENTS

In Loving Memory
of Daquin Antonio Bastian
1981–2011

This manuscript was shelved for more than a decade. During its completion, I lost my oldest son. This causes many parents to search, especially spiritually.

I dedicate this book with all its wonders to my deceased son, Daquin.

THE PREFACE

In the beginning, before creation, there was a spiritual cell. The light that shone from it was dazzling and brighter than the sun. It had an immeasurable source of energy capable of sustaining all its needs. This cell was a god.

God created a spiritual community and placed many creations within him. These creations eventually self-destructed due to their evilness. Therefore, god was alone, as he was in the beginning.

Although his first creations were destroyed by evil, he created other creations with different limitations and vowed not to allow his entire creation to be destroyed by evil again. Each creation had a distinct form and purpose. Some creations were created with a free will to do good, and others were created without this free will because their purpose was to serve.

Evil also became a foreign force in the cell because it opposed the will of god. This force was initiated as a result of the interactions of the creatures with free will.

Evil hindered the operation of the cell and inflicted suffering on the gods. Even some of the angels whose function was to serve were eventually given free will so they could be tested by the evil one.

God made known the punishment for evil, and he instituted a redemption plan for those who committed evil and desired to repent. This redemption plan required the angels to pay penance in the form of trials and tribulations and to resist evil.

A place was prepared for this process, and a ransom had to be paid to free the angels. Because there was no one qualified to become the ransom for the evil angels, god fell into creation in order to redeem the angels who repented in their hearts but remained hostages to the evil one.

Acknowledgments

Special thanks to my many draft readers who made positive contributions to the completion of this book: Howard P. Bastian, Rhonda Thurston-Ingraham, Lolitta Marshall Rolle, and Clyde W. Sawyer.

INTRODUCTION

The Cell of the Gods takes the reader on a spiritual journey beyond the physical world as it is known, into a world that is only imaginable through metaphors. This book will stimulate the reader's thinking and imagination with the possibilities of the beginning of time.

The Cell of the Gods explains the mystery of a god. It highlights the challenges the god encounters with his creations, namely the infiltration of evil into a world that was created for good.

The author brilliantly illustrates how the spiritual world was divided by evil and war. It explains what was required by the god to conquer evil, redeem his angels, and restore his cell.

The Beginning

A lone, flickering light appeared in the midst of nothing. It had scars and was weary. It was a light that was full of grief and sorrow; the rays were short and dim. It was the lone survivor of an advanced spiritual community.

This community was created for good and was to be sustained by good. Evil somehow penetrated it and became cancerous, slowly devouring the good. The evil forces developed hardened hearts and, because of their evilness, could not perceive their own self-destruction although the warnings of deterioration appeared.

The once-luminous light of a singular cell transmitted multi-coloured rays. Each colour of the rays was a source of life support for a creation. These rays were eventually hindered and darkened by evil, and the creatures could not function to their full capacity.

This cell was divided into four sections. The top was the Ancient One's abode—he was the source from which all life stemmed. In the second section lived the god of instruction, who received all instructions from the Ancient One and transmitted them to the god of creation in the third section who created or formed all things according to the instructions received. The fourth section was occupied by the god of sanctification, who activated the instructions or placed life into creation. These gods resided in an environment of pure good and were capable of eternally sustaining their survival.

The gods, although they appeared to be separate and to perform distinct duties, always acted in unison with one force. On extraordinary occasions, they combined themselves into one god who was capable of performing more than the duties of all of the separate gods.

A fifth section, which was located at the bottom of the cell, was created for all creations. All the creations had some traits that were similar to those of the gods and were sustained by the rays that shone from the Ancient One.

This section became enormous because god provided other creations for their enjoyment.

The entire gigantic, triangular cell operated in unison until some of the creations realized that they had free will to make decisions and to choose their destiny. This section of the cell soon became chaotic.

Some of the creations used their free will to do evil and threaten their eternal status. Soon, the evilness caused some of the brilliant lights that stemmed from god to grow dim and, in some cases, darken. As a result, this section was divided into two parts—evil and good—as each group campaigned for its beliefs and forcefully fought for dominion.

God sent his messengers to teach his doctrine to his creation to deter them from committing evil. As a result of the creations that had become hard-hearted in their evil actions, a loud sound was heard for the first time in this spiritual community. It was a great explosion that destroyed the good and the evil creations. The entire fifth section of the trianglular cell was destroyed and detached from the cell of god.

The remaining part of the cell incurred scars and wounds, and the light of the Ancient One became dim because of the enormous energy that was lost during the destruction. The Ancient One vowed to himself that he would not destroy the good and the evil again. The gods became one because there were no creations to be sustained.

THE NEW COMMUNITY

The Ancient One revitalized the forces within him, and as a result the darkness was eliminated and pure brilliant rays once again stemmed from his eternal cell. There was no creation, space, or time inside his eternal cell. Nothing existed outside the cell because the cell was the only thing that existed. Therefore, evil could not exist because there was no conflict.

The Ancient One had the ability to imagine and sustain everything in eternal coexistence. This power and the mystery of the cell were known only by him. In his humility and wisdom, he again divided his cell into four functioning parts, each of which became a deity. Although they were a part of the Ancient One, they also worshipped him.

Due to the Ancient One's love and esteem of himself, he unselfishly utilized his imagination and systematically extended his cell to again include a fifth section. This section was created to contain his creation. He imagined his creation, and the god who resided in the second section gave his instruction to the god in the third section, who designed the creation. And the god in the fourth section sanctified them, and they became living creatures.

The skies, clouds, waters, and fire appeared in the Ancient One's cell with its beauty and splendour as if it had always existed. The clouds formed the pathways, the skies stretched endlessly, and the waters and fire became the gods' special instruments.

The seas and rivers appeared, full of fishes, mammals, and other creatures, and each of them had a different spirit and purpose in eternity.

Then the mountains, hills, plains, and valleys appeared, furnished with trees, plants, grass, and vegetation. The cattle, beasts, creeping things, and birds moved upon them. The wolf and the lamb played and slept together, while the leopard lay down with the kid. And the calf, bear, and lion walked together and ate hay with the ox. The adder was just another harmless reptile because there was no hunger, sickness, or death in eternity.

As the creations initially appeared, they were in awe and in wonder. They knew that they were a gift created by the Ancient One because of his relationship with them. Each of them was connected to his cell by a ray of light that sustained them. The Ancient One marvelled at his creation and was content.

Each creation, although attached to the Ancient One's cell, was unrestricted and enjoyed the freedom in an environment where there was no place or space. All the creations were equal as they served their purposes with enthusiasm, moved about, and communicated with one another.

The Ancient One also created sons and daughters, and he placed a heart and free will within each of them because they were made in his image. Each of his children was given portions of his character, such as truth, love, grace, wisdom, knowledge, understanding, and humility. They were created to be his stewards and were to use the different gifts assigned to them to enhance his cell. Their responsibility was to serve him and the other creations.

They also were able to exist within their own imaginations, but they could not create. The traits given to them by the Ancient One allowed them to work in unison to achieve whatever they desired.

The fifth section of the Ancient One's cell became very active as his children intermingled among themselves and the other creations. The sounds of fun and laughter from this section were very comforting to the Ancient One, who resided in the first section of the triangular cell.

The Ancient One was pleased with his creations and decided to create angels to serve him in his domain. These angels were different from the children because they did not have hearts, free will, or their own imaginations. They existed in the Ancient One's imagination, and their purpose was to worship and to be of service to him.

THE TEMPLE

The children's free will allowed them to live within their own imaginations; therefore, there were no restrictions upon them. The Ancient One visited and served them, and he intermingled with them although they were also attached to the rays from his cell. In order to make himself more accessible to his creation, he built a temple on the top of the highest mountain between the fourth and the fifth section of the cell.

On this mountain were gardens, vineyards, cattle, farms, and forests to supply the sacrifices and to sustain the temple with all its needs such as flowers, fruits, and herbs. The temple also had its water, fire, and clouds assigned to it.

Some of the angels were given special gifts to make the temple's furnishings, artworks, utensils, musical instruments, altars, tables, seats, candlesticks, shovels, bowls, spoons, basins, and fire pans. The musical instruments, such as the trumpet, harp, cymbal, organ, and stringed instruments, were assigned to special angels.

The walls surrounding the temple were made of several layers of precious stones that had been taken from the mountains. There were four gigantic open gates attached to the huge gateposts located at the sides of the temple. Each gate had an outer and an inner court that led to a bronze altar. The temple was constantly lit by the rays that emanated from the Ancient One.

The pavements in the outer courtyards were made of silver and were surrounded with palm and olive trees. The seats in the courtyards were made with wood from selected trees of the forest. Several steps of clear crystal led up from each of the outer courts and into the inner courts.

Pillars of bronze lined the inner courtyards, trimmed at the top with carvings of pomegranates and olive and palm tree branches. The floors were filled with white clouds. In the courtyards were tables and seats hewn from stones, and in the middle of each of the four courtyards was a bronze altar with utensils. Leading up from room where the altar was located in the four inner courts were seven golden steps to the center courts.

A cloud surrounded the center courts. The four center courts with their chambers and large winding corridors merged at the only golden altar below the sanctuary. The golden altar was furnished with golden utensils and seats.

From the middle of the golden altar, living waters and fire flowed throughout the temple. The water supplied food for the gifts—such as grace, wisdom, knowledge, and understanding—that were planted in chosen soil around the riverbeds to be given to whomever the Ancient One chose. And the fire that flowed out from the altar sanctified all his creation. The golden altar was enclosed with a veil made from a brilliant light.

Directly behind the eastern side of the golden altar were nine steps that extended up to the sanctuary. At the highest point in the sanctuary, there was a seat for the Ancient One. The huge doorposts and the door of the sanctuary were made from a variety of beautiful stones that glittered in the incense that appeared to constantly fall down the sanctuary steps.

After completing the temple, the Ancient One created temple angels and archangels to serve in and perform the duties in the temple. The talents given to the archangels gave them more seniority than the children. These angels were the Ancient One's messengers, and they were responsible for supervising the other angels.

Temple creatures were created and restricted to perform duties in the temple. The sanctuary angels and beasts were created to minister to the Ancient One and to praise and serve him in the sanctuary. The sanctuary restricted all other creations from entering its chamber if they were not created to do so.

The Ancient One also bestowed special gifts upon the angels he chose to design and make the splendid, colourful garments. These garments were appropriately trimmed with complementing ornaments for ceremonial and normal uses for the angels and children.

As the Ancient One moved about the temple in his glory, a mist of incense encircled him and the magnificent royal train that trailed him. The temple's atmosphere was always one of majesty as the children and angels continuously kneeled, bowed, and praised him as they felt the mystery and the incomprehensible aura of him in his magnificent temple.

THE EVIL ONE

The children interacted among themselves except for two sons who stayed close to the temple, around the golden altar in front of the sanctuary, rather than exploring or interacting with their siblings. They were in constant, direct contact with the Ancient One, and as a result of their commitment, they learned and understood more than the others about their father.

One of the two sons soon infiltrated a part of the sanctuary that was restricted from them. This son perfected whatever task he performed and became full of arrogant pride. This trait of arrogant pride was foreign to the cell and became known as evil, and it negatively affected the relationship between the Ancient One and his creation.

The evil son, unbeknownst to his siblings, competed for his father's love. Because of his father's impartiality regarding his children, the evil son eventually developed anger, hatred, malice, vengeance, and selfishness toward his siblings, resulting in tensions, arguments, and confrontation among the children.

The children were created with similarities to the Ancient One, with free will to do good. The evil son did not seek help or discuss his unnatural feelings toward his father or siblings. He began to direct actions of jealousy toward the brother who also stayed around the golden altar and was full of humility. He kept the thoughts to himself and allowed them to negatively affect his relationship with his brother and eventually his other siblings.

Soon, the evil son began to influence some of the other siblings with his negative feelings for his brother. Although some of the children sought their father's counsel on this matter, eventually the children were divided and the Ancient One's cell was threatened by the evil son's doctrine, whose heart had become hardened.

The two brothers who stayed around the altar were soon recognized as leaders of the forces of good and evil. The siblings aligned themselves with the brother of their choice. The arguments and confrontations advanced to abusive words and attacks. Then, the rivalry between the groups elevated to the point where the evil brother attempted to injure his counterpart. The result of this action was suffering and pain introduced into the cell.

The evil son was very talented, and he maximized his potential, working to understand most of the workings, mysteries, and wonders of his father. Because of his close relationship with him, he felt as if he were more powerful than all the other siblings and creation.

He became aware that he had emptied his heart of humility and replaced it with an arrogant pride that had hardened his heart and darkened some of the brilliant rays that emanated from his father. He continuously justified his actions and was unaware that he was on a path of self-destruction.

The Ancient One hated the evil that his son did but loved and admired his ability to perform his work with perfection. He also observed the respect that his son received from his siblings. The evil son continued to plant evil seeds in the cell, but because he was full of arrogant pride, it became difficult for him to seek or receive advice. Eventually he misled some of his siblings with half truths and outright lies. His father allowed the evil to take its course; however, because of the magnitude of some cases, he intervened.

The evil son began to watch with envy the service and the worship that his siblings, the angels, and the rest of creation gave to his father. Soon, he developed a desire to become like his father and was confident that he could perform the signs, wonders, mysteries, and other workings of the cell.

He also felt betrayed by his father and became further enraged and angry with his brother after he learned that his father had allowed his brother to supervise a part of the temple. Feeling insecure, he waited for an opportunity to murder his brother.

He eventually murdered his brother on the golden altar below the sanctuary in the midst of the spirits of all creation. The cell of the Ancient One for the first time wept because the act of murder was unnatural. The Ancient One was saddened by how his son had used his free will to commit such heinous evil. The entire cell suffered immensely because of this act of violence, and the rays from the Ancient One noticeably darkened.

The cell retaliated for this violent action, and a portion of it became inflicted with famine and plagues; some of the creation died because the natural sequence had been disrupted. The harvest of the crops in certain areas decreased. Some of the creations began to display unnatural, aggressive behaviours because of the lack of an element to which they had become accustomed.

The evil son did not have the potential or the ability to even envision how he had been created and fully understand the mysteries of his father, yet his evil thoughts blinded him and he foolishly felt secure, believing that he was next in line to control his father's cell.

He never forgave his father for allowing his brother to supervise a part of the temple. Therefore, he made preparations to challenge him for full control of the temple and the entire cell.

The evil son masqueraded as someone who had the potential and capability to operate the working of the cell in the best interest of everyone. He increased his campaign to convince all of his siblings to disrespect his father. He deliberately visited the angels and other creations more frequently and became more intimate with them. He dialogued with them and questioned their conversations with the Ancient One.

Because of the spirits that had been assigned to the angels and their lack of free will, the evil son was unable to cause them to become evil. But he succeeded in tempting some of the angels to perform their duties ineffectively, and as a result, these angels were considered to be disobedient.

The Ancient One punished and chastised the disobedient angels but allowed them to continue their service. The evil one was not satisfied with tempting the angels to become disobedient; he wanted to claim the angels as his own and to tempt them to perform evil.

He then requested that his father remove the protection from around the angels so that he could test them with evil to determine whom they would serve. The removal of the protection meant that the angels would become similar to the children and have free will.

THE CHOICE

Although the Ancient One knew the evil thoughts before they entered the hearts of his children, he allowed the evil to develop into maturity so that he could destroy it in its entirety. He was grieved and saddened that it had penetrated his holy temple and left an indelible mark on the golden altar. He also watched and marvelled at the wickedness that the evil son concocted in his heart as the Ancient One endured vicious attacks from him and some of his siblings.

Because of the Ancient One's high esteem and his unconditional love for the angels, he decided to allow them the opportunity to receive free will. He also instituted through his grace a redemption plan for the angels who would be deceived by the evil one and would wish to return to his doctrine.

His children did not have this opportunity for redemption because they were created with hearts to do good and given free will; therefore, those who chose evil were warned that they were destined for destruction.

The body of the Ancient One came to a standstill as he communicated his original purpose for the angels, which was to serve, worship, and obey him. Then the Ancient One told the angels about the evil son's request for him to give them free will to do good in order to be tested by the evil one.

He gave them the option of continuing in their original state or accepting free will to do good and possibly evil, and he also warned them of the consequences. They were told how the god who resided in the fourth section of the cell would again sanctify them in their new role if they chose free will.

When he was satisfied that all the angels understood their original relationship with him and the proposed state of free will, he removed the protective shield of sanctification from around them and released them from his imagination to allow them to decide whether or not they wanted free will or to continue in their original state.

All the angels were positioned in front of him, and one by one they chose to either stand at his right to accept their current status or at his left to receive free will.

After all the angels had made their choice, those on his right hand were reinstalled and sanctified to continue with their original relationship. Those on his left accepted a relationship similar to that of his sons and daughters. They were sanctified and given free will and hearts to account for their actions.

Some of the angels who chose free will adjusted their work habits and their style of worship as they performed their duties. They were removed from the temple because the Ancient One had vowed that evil would not be committed in his temple again.

The evil son and his evil siblings immediately began to frequent the angels to strengthen their relationships with them. The followers of the evil son staged an intense campaign against the Ancient One through slanderous remarks and propaganda, and they criticized his administration of the angels and his description of evil. They also accused him of being selfish in demanding that his angels serve, obey, and worship him. At the end of each of the evil son's intense campaigns, he promised the angels a new structure in the cell in which their conditions would be improved.

The angels' evil actions placed darkness around their hearts and eventually hindered the transmission of some of the rays from the Ancient One. Therefore, they did not receive the full wisdom, knowledge, understanding, and grace.

Soon, a raging battle began between the Ancient One and his evil son for the heart of each angel who had chosen free will. Some of the angels who had chosen not to continue in their original state immediately accepted the evil son's slander and propaganda, while others pondered his doctrine. Others outright rejected the evil son's doctrine and continued in the path of good.

The followers of the evil son gradually increased in number as he lied to the angels and spread his propaganda. Therefore, the relationship between the angels slowly changed. Many of them engaged in debates on good and evil. These debates bred quarrels and sometimes became aggressive and abusive toward the angels who refused evil.

Angels that belonged to the same units were in some cases violently separated on these issues. The relationships among them further deteriorated as the evil angels' work decreased they expected the good angels to assist them with their daily allotment of work. Eventually, the good angels were persecuted and even forced to worship the Ancient One in secret to avoid confrontation.

The evil angels became more adamant as they discussed the evil son's plan at their meetings under the hills and deep in the mountains. On occasions when the evil son visited them, he practiced his witchcraft to convince them that he had the same powers as his father. After the meetings, his followers returned to their normal places of work and homes with more determination to spread his doctrine.

As the Ancient One sat in his sanctuary, he observed his creation and the continuous evil that they committed against him, inflicting pain and suffering to his cell. He heard the cries and the prayers of his faithful angels and children and the murdered angels and children in the golden altar who also cried out to him to restore his cell.

Because of his concern for the angels that chose free will, he visited them, but the ones with hardened, evil hearts could not stand in his presence because of his goodness and glory. They observed from a distance. During his visits, he always encouraged the angels to choose good over evil and to respond with love to their counterparts.

The Entrapment

It was very easy for the evil one to manipulate some of the angels who had received free will. He was created with a heart and free will, and he had spent a lot of time in the presence of his father, learning about the mysteries of creation. He pretended to display the traits of his father as he approached and befriended the angels and appeared to be concerned for their welfare. Therefore, at the beginning of the angels' association with him, he appeared to have a paternal relationship with them. After he gained their confidence, he presented his propaganda and slowly lowered them into his trap.

The evil one continued to enter the presence of his father after some of the angels had obtained free will. He also attempted to infiltrate the group of angels that remained in the temple with his doctrine but was unaware that his father had removed those who had chosen free will. Therefore, it was impossible to distract them from performing their duties.

The evil one was satisfied that he had successfully disrupted the operations and the functions of the cell by convincing some of the children and angels from every area of service to follow him. Then he became confident and wanted to defy his father openly. He planned a huge ceremony on a mountaintop, where everyone saw his followers voluntarily let him place his mark upon them. After the indelible mark was placed upon their hearts, he told them that it represented his ownership.

The evil son's cult consisted of two parts: the charming and glamorous side that was presented to the potential followers, and the second part that included the slave camps, which were kept secret by his dedicated angels. He subtly placed his new recruits in groups to campaign for his cause, and then he slowly placed demands upon them to succeed.

Soon they realized the harsh punishment that resulted from their failure, sometimes determining whether they would be placed into a slave camp. All of the angels in camps, at one time or another, performed services for the evil one, which included inflicting evil against his father. Some of the angels who found themselves in these camps wanted to re-establish their relationships with the Ancient One. Ironically, the evil angels who were not in these camps continued to degrade the enslaved ones.

The evil son continuously encouraged the angels to follow him, and he intimidated the ones who chose to do good rather than evil. He boasted to his evil followers about his power to delay the angels' requests from reaching the golden altar where the Ancient One interacted with his creation. And he made a mockery of them as he tried to convince them that they were worthless and abandoned by their creator.

He also appointed a beast, which he controlled, to oversee the affairs of the camp and make certain that his wishes were followed. Then he openly told the angels in the camp that they must serve him alone because he controlled their destiny.

Despite the evil one's aggressive campaign, some of the angels repented and rededicated themselves to the Ancient One as they recognized the evil son as a tyrant who was not interested in their personal welfare but only in their ability to attack their creator. Although they repented, they remained under the evil one's control.

These rededicated angels were violently assaulted by the evil one and his followers because they insulted his arrogant pride by refusing to obey him. He was determined to break them at all cost and use them as an example to others.

The evil son and his followers and slaves built seven shrines to honor him in strategic locations throughout the fifth section of the cell. Each of the shrines represented and supported a specific evil that was an abomination to the Ancient One.

The evil son's followers, depending upon their level of evil, were assigned to a particular shrine. As they perfected these various evils, they were elevated to other shrines that indulged in a higher degree of evil, ranging from one to seven. The evil one also appointed seven of the archangels who had become evil to be his high priests and administrators in these shrines. The shrines were set up in a manner similar to that of the Ancient One's temple, but it had idols that were filled with the evil son's spirits and used to practice witchcraft.

The Impersonator

The evil one became very confident that he was powerful and knowledgeable enough to succeed his father. With confidence, he gathered his followers to the shrine on a mountain to serve and worship him. Then he insisted that his followers obey the beast. From that moment, the evil one became known as Ramis because he thought that he had elevated himself to the status of his father.

He frequently visited his followers in the mountain, vineyards, skies, farms, and other places. During these visits, he encouraged his followers to commit the seven evils against his father. These evils were constantly in his father's presence; as a result, the entire cell suffered, particularly the creation in the fifth section because the rays that they depended on for their livelihood were weakened because of the evil they committed. Although the evildoers were deprived, they rejoiced in what appeared to be a malfunction in the cell.

Ramis also visited the angels that chose to be good to tempt them to become evil as he continuously slandered the name of his father and shared portions of the truth with them. He wanted to bring his father to shame as he emerged as the undisputable ruler. His desire was to ultimately control the Ancient One's temple because it represented authority.

This was a period in which the supremacy of the Ancient One was furiously attacked and his power to defend his creation questioned. His spirit continued to work with those who opened their hearts, and they received his gift of wisdom, knowledge, understanding, and grace.

The Ancient One continued to feel the evil that was committed and the cries and the sufferings of his angels who were in Ramis's slave camps and deprived of the free will he had given them. He eventually sent his messengers to ask Ramis to free the angels, but Ramis insisted that the angels were his property and that he needed them to facilitate his needs, the needs of his followers, and the operation of the shrines. After Ramis finished his discussion with his father's messengers, he told his beast to increase the slaves' workload and to tempt them to commit evil acts against his father and punish them if necessary.

Ramis knew that a war with his father was inevitable, so he intensified his campaign without informing his newly recruited angels that they would eventually fight against their creator. He and his followers did whatever was necessary to gain the angels' loyalty. They also began to intensify their abuse and sometimes murdered the angels who did not accept the doctrine of Ramis.

Ramis deceived his followers by using witchcraft to appear to be like his father because he was aware that he was unable to create or restore creation. He felt confident that his use of witchcraft would assist him in defeating his father. He also prepared his seven shrines for confrontation with the Ancient One because he knew that his father loved his creation but hated the evil that they committed. Therefore, he was certain that his father would confront the seven evils in each of the shrines.

All of Ramis's followers prepared themselves for war, and most of them abandoned their normal abodes and workplaces to help around the shrines. The angels in the shrine continuously performed their ceremonies and rituals to control the outcome of war. Various forms of witchcraft were also practiced around the altars in the shrines as testimony of Ramis's power and to strengthen the beliefs of his followers.

Ramis summoned all his shrines' beasts and high priests to the seventh shrine as he convened the war council so they could create strategies for fighting his father's army, attacking the temple, destroying his father, and controlling the cell.

Meanwhile, the activity level around the Ancient One's temple also increased as the angels became busy performing their services while also actively preparing the temple and its altars to offer continuous sacrifices. In and around the temple were choirs of angels who played their instruments and danced within the Ancient One's imagination.

As the fragrant aroma from the burnt offerings on the altars in the temple entered the Ancient One's sanctuary, he was compelled to deal with the requests of the faithful to redeem the angels in Ramis's slave camps where they were denied their free will to do good or evil.

The gift of free will was the basis of the angels' existence; therefore, Ramis's tampering with it affected the basis for their repentance and their final judgement. This was viewed by the Ancient One as an evil and a hindrance to his plans.

As a result of the evil, the rays from the Ancient One's body that flowed through the golden altar to all creation to assist them in functioning to their full capacity were contaminated. Therefore, the golden altar had to be constantly covered by the rituals and sacrifices of the faithful to temporarily wash the evil from the altar as they praised and worshiped the Ancient One.

As the evil increased and the pain and suffering in Ramis's slave camps intensified, the covering of the evil on the alter became exceedingly difficult. Soon, the veil of pure light around the golden altar became impassable; no one was able to enter the chamber of the golden altar.

Ramis was aware of the effect that his evil had on the golden altar chamber, so he continued to intensify his evil practices and increased his holding of slaves.

He felt very powerful as he boasted about his control over his faithful and enslaved angels and how he diminished the glory of his father and the cell. He was also prepared to degrade and manipulate his father further by requesting that he become a co-ruler of the cell.

THE CHOSEN ONE

Evil was a foreign force that was not created by the Ancient One, yet he prepared a way for the evil angels to have an opportunity to repent. He patiently endured the suffering from the evil in his cell as he allowed it to mature to its fullness. He was very concerned about the enslaved angels who wanted to serve him. He also took into consideration the process that would eventually destroy evil. He knew that if he directly commanded the evildoers to repent and they refused, they would be destroyed instantly because his direct command could not be compromised.

For this reason, he chose to appoint someone to confront Ramis, repeatedly if necessary, on his behalf in order to obtain the release of the enslaved angels.

In the sanctuary, the Ancient One sat alone in the mist of the clouds. Suddenly, he disappeared and three deities appeared. These are the gods that occupied the second, third, and fourth sections of the cell. They had been summoned to discuss the redemption plan and the restoration of the cell.

They decided to appoint someone to champion the cause of the redemption process. They scrutinized all of children who remained faithful in order to select one of them to be responsible for redeeming the fallen angels.

None of the remaining good children qualified for the task because Ramis had murdered most of those who were capable of performing such a task. But the gods insisted that the evil one must be confronted in order to facilitate the release of the angels.

It was decided that one of the gods would fall into creation as an angel. He had to fall into the body of an archangel, a son, and finally an angel. This meant that a co-creator would become a creation for the sole purpose of freeing the angels.

The god of sanctification, who resided in the fourth section, cried out, saying that he would go to redeem the angels. The Ancient One was pleased that a part of himself would become his chosen linage to conquered evil and to redeem his angels.

The Ancient One was stripped of some of his power as a part of him fell into creation to fight against evil. Because of this transition, the Ancient One was unable to perform some of his duties because the composite of the gods was incomplete.

He waited with anticipation for the god of sanctification, who had become his special messenger, to defeat evil and return as a god after he restored the cell as it had been in the beginning.

The redemption plan was passed to the god of sanctification in the sanctuary. As he sat in his chair, he fell from his glory into the body of an archangel, and then the spirit of the archangel left him and he became a son of god.

The angels on the nine steps of the sanctuary blew the trumpets, and the choirs around the four bronze and the golden altars sang the same song simultaneously. The children and angels who had died and been placed in the golden altar awoke, while the captives in Ramis's camp rejoiced because the rays from the Ancient One made them aware of the redemption plan and the restoration of the cell.

From the step of the sanctuary, the archangel summoned Ramis to the temple on behalf of the chosen son. Ramis was dumbfounded because he was not aware of a son of the Ancient One who had the power to summon him. The name made him feel threatened because he thought that after he had murdered several of his brothers, he was the only son eligible to inherit the cell of the Ancient One. So he and his two beasts immediately rushed to the temple out of curiosity, putting aside their battle plans.

As Ramis entered the temple, an invisible force stopped his beasts from following him. He quickly went to his seat at the golden altar, where the archangels stood dressed in their ceremonial robes and ornaments and the incense, with its sweet smell, floated down the nine steps from the sanctuary to the golden altar.

Also in the inner court and around the bronze altars were angels dressed in their robes as they too waited. Even the angels who adorned the heavens directed their attention to the temple. The angels, the children, and all creation that were not participating in Ramis's evil focused on the events around the golden altar. Ramis and his followers, because of their evil, could not receive the full rays of knowledge that would enable them to understand the events that were about to unfold.

Then, suddenly, the chosen son began to descend from the sanctuary, and the angels and children around the golden altar prostrated themselves below to give honor to him. As the cloud from around the platform outside the sanctuary lifted, two gods appeared.

As the chosen son reached the platform below the nine steps, he looked up toward the gods and led the worshippers below in prostrating themselves before the gods.

As the chosen son completed the honors to the deities, Ramis was dumbfounded. He realized that the son had an intimate relationship with them because he had come down from the steps of the sanctuary that were restricted to the children. Ramis instantly began to think about his succession to rule the cell and the possibility of its being jeopardized by the chosen son. He became even more insecure, defensive, and determined to challenge the Ancient One.

Suddenly, the glory of the chosen son surrounded Ramis, and he covered his evil heart with his garment. The son instructed Ramis to free the captives and to allow them to practice their free will. He also asked Ramis to release the angels he held hostage and to remove all the evil from the cell.

Ramis became furious as he realized that the Ancient One had endorsed the communication of the son. He became very adamant, insisting that his angels had voluntarily accepted his mark upon their hearts and therefore he had the authority to do whatever he wanted with them, adding that he had no intentions to release any. With laughter he responded to the second demand to leave the cell of the Ancient One that he was convinced he controlled.

The hearts of the children and the angels who had accepted free will and abided by the Ancient One's doctrine were filled with chants and singing because they knew that the plan for the restoration of the cell and the redemption plan for the angels were activated. Ramis then stormed out of the temple to continue to prepare for war.

As the son prepared to leave the temple, he placed and lit seven golden candlesticks upon the golden altar. These candlesticks were to be a reminder to the Ancient One of the restriction he had placed upon himself to avoid entering the chamber of the sanctuary until evil was conquered and the enslaved angels who were Ramis's hostages in the seven shrines were freed. Then a rainbow appeared above the golden altar as the deities watched from the platform in front of the sanctuary.

THE MESSENGER

The chosen son prepared to visit the seven shrines in an attempt to confront Ramis and gain the release of the captives. As the clouds cleared around the son, who was on the golden altar, he was transformed into a lion with wings upon walking through the candlesticks on the golden altar. Then, suddenly, the lion lifted from the altar with its powerful wings and flew toward the first of Ramis's seven shrines.

The lion landed on the platform of the first shrine, where the angels defiled their garments by uttering disrespectful words against the Ancient One. Then, the protective, glittering seal placed upon him by the deities engulfed the young lion as it climbed a huge step before entering the shrine.

The worshippers around the altar had just simultaneously finished prostrating themselves before an idol that looked like a frog. These worshippers consisted of new converts who had committed their first evil act against the Ancient One. This shrine was similar to the others in that it had a slave camp that consisted of offenders who did not perform their duties or worship Ramis.

The young lion entered the dark shrine as the high priest was about to offer the blood ritual. The lion made his way in a straight line to the altar as the worshippers took steps to remove themselves from his path and covered their hearts because of his glory. As the young lion approached the altar, an old frog appeared and leapt upon the altar, disrespecting the name of the Ancient One.

The worshippers observed with interest the reactions of the young lion and the old frog. Suddenly, the old frog was transformed into an onrushing bear, and the chosen son emerged from the body of the young lion.

The son told Ramis, who was in the form of a bear, to "let the angels in the slave camp go." Ramis refused the request, and in his anger, he used his witchcraft in an attempt to inflict injury upon the son. The son blocked Ramis's spell and used it to instead destroy a part of the shrine. Then the son began to share the doctrine of the Ancient One with those who were present. Some of the angels who witnessed the sharing of the doctrine became susceptible to the word.

Then the son left the shrine in the same manner in which he had arrived. As he reappeared on the golden altar, the wings of the lion blew out one of the seven candlesticks.

Over time, the son delivered his message to the next four shrines, each having an additional step at its entrance to climb that represented the level of evil. Ramis's followers became more hostile as the son visited in an ascending order the shrines, which became darker. The worshippers, according to the extent of the hardening of their hearts, moved closer to the son as he entered the respective shrines.

The message of the son was the same, and Ramis's responses were consistent with his first. He confronted Ramis in these shrines in the form of a leopard, fly, cobra, and goat. Some of the angels in the shrine became susceptible to the Ancient One's doctrine.

When the son visited Ramis's sixth shrine, he landed as an eagle on the platform below the six huge steps. The members of the sixth shrine indulged in six evils against the Ancient One, which were as follows: disrespect of his name, lust, jealousy, blasphemy, lies, and murder. These angels showed absolutely no remorse for their evil. Somehow they were convinced that their actions were right. As the eagle entered the shrine, the darkness was like a thick shield; the eagle's beak became a flaming torch that penetrated the darkness. And the eagle used its strong wings to hold off the aggressive attack from the shrine's worshippers.

The beast that was in charge of the shrine reluctantly stopped the high priest from offering the sacrifices to Ramis and immediately proceeded to meet the eagle, who was making his way to the altar. Suddenly, the beast was transformed into a dragon, and the son emerged from the body of the eagle. The son again delivered the same message to Ramis, to "let the angels in the slave camps go." Ramis again did not heed the message of the son.

The angels present were amazed at the power of the son as they felt the sharing of the doctrine, but none of them became susceptible to the word of the Ancient One because their hearts were hardened.

Ramis himself resided within the seventh shrine. He prepared his shrine and members for the expected visit of the son. Members of his army were stationed for the first time outside around the shrine to prevent the son from entering. Two sentinels were stationed both outside and inside the doors, which were closed. Ramis did not know when the son would visit, nor did he know the form in which the son would appear, but he was certain that he would come to deliver his message to the seventh shrine.

Ramis continued to use his witchcraft to determine the time that the son would arrive so that he and his followers would be ready to murder him. They convinced themselves that sufficient precautions were taken around the shrine so they would be notified in advance of the arrival. Therefore, they continued to feast and commit all of the seven evils, including bowing down and worshipping Ramis, which was an abomination to the Ancient One.

Suddenly, there was a great sound of thunder for the first time in the cell, followed by lightning that came from the temple of the Ancient One.

The one remaining lit candle on the golden altar was blown out by the swirling wind that transported the son on the tip of a lightning bolt to Ramis's seventh shrine. The door of the shrine was struck open, and the son appeared inside it as a calf. The heavy darkness inside the shrine slowed the movement of the calf, while Ramis and his sibling were able to move about freely. The worshippers were mesmerized by the bright halo around the head of the calf.

The son emerged from the calf sharing the Ancient One's doctrine with the angels in the shrine, whom he paralysed and forced to listen to his words. Then Ramis and his sibling attempted to murder the son, but the Ancient One's covering protected him. The request was again put to Ramis to "let the angels in the slave camp go." Ramis not only said no, but he again claimed ownership of his angels based upon their voluntary decision to have his mark placed upon themselves. After the son left the shrine, the angels with hardened hearts regretted only not having been able to murder him.

The son took with him the murdered angels and children of the Ancient One that had been held as Ramis's prizes to display his powers to his followers.

Ramis acknowledged that he was not effective against the son during his visits to his shrines, but he boasted about how the glory of the Ancient One was diminished because of his evil and how it affected the veil around the golden altar. And he further assured himself of how powerless the Ancient One was in gaining the release of the slaves in his camp.

Therefore, with confidence he continued to look forward to the war against the Ancient One as he strengthened the protection around his only prized possession—the slaves whom he spitefully oppressed in order to keep the attention of the Ancient One.

THE WAR

The angels and children sat outside the veil that encompasses the golden altar, mourning because it had become impassable due to the evil that it had absorbed from the cell. The evil also interrupted the flow of communication to the golden altar; even the requests of the faithful angels and children were delayed in reaching the temple.

The altar was the central point that received communications from all creation and transmitted them to the Ancient One's chamber in the sanctuary. Therefore, the archangels rerouted the communications to and from the sanctuary through the bronze altars.

Ramis became convinced that his army was large and powerful enough to overthrow the army of the Ancient One. So he gathered his army from the seven shrines to march them against the temple. His beast who was the commander in charge led the army. The legions from the seven shrines lined up in ascending order according to their shrine numbers to march into battle. The slaves from all of the shrines were placed behind the legions from the seventh shrine as hostages.

The squadron of chariots led the army, followed by knights on their pale horses of white, red, and black and dressed in their battle attire. The riders wore coats of mail and greaves of metal upon their legs, and they carried swords, lances, spears, or bows. The foot soldiers wore their helmets and shoulder, leg, and breast protective gear. They carried weapons such as swords, axes, and spears.

Ramis identified a strategic spot on a mountain where he and one of his beasts could view the temple and the progression of his army. He also prepared an apparatus to perform his witchcraft to assist his army in battle. He knew that the first two legions would be slaughtered because they would be unable to compete against the army of the Ancient One.

The Ancient One and the gods meditated as they watched Ramis's army in their minds, preparing to climb the mountain to attack the temple. Then the god of instruction gave the battle plan to the chosen son to execute. The Ancient One could not act to his full potential because the god of sanctification had fallen from the deity to become a creation in the form of the chosen son.

The chosen son and the archangel selected the soldiers' uniforms and weapons. They had the same uniforms, protective gear, and weapons as Ramis's army except that the colour of the uniforms was gold and the weapons were made with gold and silver. The golden chariots with their blazing fire and triangular golden flags were pulled by well-groomed white, red, and black horses dressed in the army's colours.

Then, suddenly, the angels dressed in their army attire took their places with their golden trumpets in the outer courts around the temple. The sounds of their trumpets were heard on one accord within the cell. As a result of the trumpet sounds, lightning and thunder proceeded from the golden altar, and earthquakes tossed huge boulders upon Ramis's army, which was climbing the mountain toward the temple.

As the earthquakes subsided, the magnificent glow from the glory of the son stunned the advancing army and brought them to a sudden halt as he and the god of instruction stood on the outer court, looking down at the casualties below the mountain.

Then, from the western mountain, parallel to where the son, the god, and his commanders stood, a thick darkness that was made up of all the evil in the cell proceeded across the battlefield toward the glow from the son. At the point where the darkness and the light clashed, both elements forcefully fought for dominion. The battlefield slowly became dim, and the angels of the Ancient One released their plague-laden horses, which flew across the battlefield into Ramis's army. Screams of pain and death followed the path of the flying horses as they made contact with Ramis's army.

The angels around the temple blew their trumpets a second time as the army entered into battle. The sounds of clashing weapons and the wheels of the rushing chariots filled the cell.

As the battle continued in the darkness, Ramis, using his witchcraft rituals, changed his army's attire so that it was similar to that of the Ancient One's army. For a brief moment, the battle ceased, and then the army of the Ancient One recognized Ramis's soldiers because they did not have the mark of light and assaulted them.

As the battle between light and darkness raged, the god of instruction strengthened the son on the outer court of the temple as he fought the rays of darkness. Ramis, with his apparatus, disrupted the communication between the commander in charge of the Ancient One's army and the Son.

The battle continued. The horses and chariots had to be abandoned, and the soldiers fought one on one as Ramis's army was forced backward into the clouds. Slowly, the light on the battlefield was restored, and the son regained his strength as he stood in the outer court of the temple, feeling the effects of the battle within him.

Then, lightning flashed in the skies, and the army of the Ancient One surrounded Ramis's army and waited for the command from the archangel. Ramis watched as a remnant of his army slowly retreated.

Upon realizing that he was losing the war, Ramis left the beast and his apparatus in a flash as he attempted to escape.

The archangel in charge of the Ancient One's army, while directing one of his regiments, recognized Ramis as he withdrew from the mountaintop. He immediately pursued Ramis and cornered him in a cleft in the rock, where he changed his appearance several times to intimidate the archangel.

Although the archangel was unable to subdue Ramis, he blocked the opening in the rock with his blazing sword to avoid Ramis from escaping until the son arrived. The son's rays overpowered Ramis and subdued him, and the archangel tied him to the rock.

The lights from the angels stationed in the skies slowly became brighter as they praised the Ancient One. The choirs of angels appeared, singing and playing music to celebrate the victory. The worshippers in the temple offered sacrifices around the bronze altars, and the veils to the golden altar returned to normalcy.

The murdered children and angels in the altars woke up praising the Ancient One, and the spirits of all creation on the altar began to move about. The angels and children who were outside the veil to the golden altar entered and took their places, praising the Ancient One.

The son placed Ramis and his soldiers in a restricted area as he and the archangel left the battlefield to return to the temple. As the son and the archangel in charge of the army entered the temple, the worshippers reverently gave the son his honors. Then the son entered an adjacent room to prepare himself before entering the chamber of the golden altar.

The son dressed in his garment and paraphernalia entered the chamber of the golden altar with the archangel walking behind him. The angels and children in the chamber prostrated themselves as the son stood between the golden altar and the steps that lead to the sanctuary, waiting to be acknowledged by the deities.

As the door of the sanctuary opened, the god of instruction and the god of creation appeared. Then, in an instant, the chosen son below reclaimed his position as the god of sanctification on the platform of the sanctuary above. The entire cell came to a standstill as the Ancient One stepped onto the platform with all his power and majesty because the three gods once again complemented the Ancient One as it had been done from the beginning.

THE SEPARATION

As the Ancient One inspected the battlefield, he found it necessary to make a dispensation in order to directly confront and talk with the evil angels. The level of evil within them determined how close they gathered around him.

He spoke with the angels about an opportunity to convert to his doctrine and to destroy the evil in their hearts. He told them that the ones who refused to destroy the evil would be separated from the cell forever.

Ramis was brought before the Ancient One in chains, and the pillars from his seven shrines rested upon him and restricted his movements. His heart was still hardened, and he refused to agree to let his slaves go.

The Ancient One communicated to Ramis that he would be separated from the cell. Then, suddenly, Ramis, his evil sibling, the beasts, the creeping things, the cattle, and the shrines went crashing into a separated cell. In this cell, each creation carried the weight of its own evilness, hindering its movements.

The Ancient One divided the angels on the battlefield into three groups: those who had rededicated themselves to the doctrine, those who remained susceptible to the doctrine, and those whose hearts were hardened.

The angels with hardened hearts were the first to be thrown out of the cell into the separate cell where Ramis had fallen. The angels who had become susceptible to his doctrine were thrown into another location, and the angels who rededicated themselves to the Ancient One were the last to leave.

The Ancient One, the children, the host of angels, and the other living things were saddened when the rededicated angels were thrown out because they would endure more suffering and pain from Ramis in the separated cell since they had chosen to serve the Ancient One.

But because Ramis had tricked, trapped, and lied to them and they had used their free will to allow Ramis to place his mark upon them, they were a part of his fraternity. Therefore, it was his option to either release them freely from his control or allow them to fight against his will of evil to determine whether or not they would continue to serve the Ancient One.

All of the angels and children who were thrown out of the cell found themselves in another cell where the evil in their hearts determined the degree of darkness that covered them. The Ancient One gave all of the inhabitants of the separated cell senses such as sight, taste, touch, smell, and hearing because they were separated from his body, which normally took care of their every need.

The inhabitants of the separate cell were vulnerable to all types of diseases, abuse, and murder, and on occasion their paraphernalia that represented their gifts from the Ancient One were stolen. Most of them became addicted to elements that they excessively abused. This was a time when the angels who believed in the doctrine of the Ancient One requested his protection during their worship to him in secret places.

A thick glass barrier separated the two cells, and no one from either cell was able to enter the other without the approval of the Ancient One.

The angels who accepted free will and had initially chosen to serve the Ancient One would participate in the final judgement of the angels in the separated cell.

The entire cell of the Ancient One was restored, renewing its brilliant rays. And all the children who remained in the cell voluntarily put upon themselves the seal of the Ancient One, vowing to do good for all eternity.

But the functioning of the cell where the Ancient One resided was not complete because a part of creation had fallen, and the requests and sacrifices for the return of the fallen angels continued in the temple.

Ramis, his beast, and the angels and children with hardened hearts soon realized that they were separated from the Ancient One. Ramis immediately establish himself as a king and set up his kingdom in the separated cell. He resumed the ceremonies in his seven shrines with more authority than he had in the cell of the Ancient One.

After his kingdom was organized in the separate cell, he and his followers began to visit the angels who had rededicated themselves and those who were susceptible to the doctrine of the Ancient One to attempt to re-establish control over them.

Although Ramis was separated from the presence of the Ancient One he prided himself on causing some angels to be thrown out with him. It was his desire to make it impossible for the Ancient One to redeem them. However, he continued to deceive them by telling them that the Ancient One did not care about their welfare and encouraged them to do evil. He also tempted the rededicated angels with gifts and other incentives in an effort to recruit them.

As a result of the defeat of Ramis's army, the archangels were able to perform their duties around the golden altar even though the veil had not fully returned to normalcy. The temple was continually full with worshippers singing, praising in their hearts, and offering sacrifices for the victory and the complete restoration of the cell.

As the Ancient One returned to his sanctuary, he was able to re-establish communications and become intimate with his creation through the golden altar.

He continued to feel the evil hearts of Ramis and the evil angels and children as he waited for his plan of redemption and judgement to be implemented, yet he was saddened that his creation that became evil had to be separated.

Because of his love and compassion, he visited the angels in the separated cell. They recognized him by his magnificent light, which was noticeable in the mist of the darkness. He observed their condition and communicated especially with the angels who had rededicated themselves and lived according to his doctrine. He gave them gifts to enhance their faith as they began their pilgrimage to their first abode.

The sight of Ramis's hostages continuously grieved the Ancient One because he was their creator and was able to solve their situation in an instant, but in humility and wisdom he allowed the angels to pay the consequences for the choices that came with free will.

The Ancient One also sent messengers into the separated cell to warn the angels of the consequences for their evil actions. Ramis was surprised at the extent of the Ancient One's concern for the welfare of these angels and worked continuously to indoctrinate them with the thought that the Ancient One did not care about their welfare.

As the angels in the separated cell heard the words of the Ancient One, more of them became susceptible to his doctrine. Ramis became enraged with them and added more burdens upon their shoulders to hinder their movements.

Ramis made a concerted effort and was successful in killing most of the Ancient One's messengers, and he used their bodies as prizes as he celebrated his powers. After the last messenger was murdered, the Ancient One again dethroned himself to allow the god of sanctification to fall into creation as an archangel and then into the body of his son to become his messenger.

The god of sanctification appeared on the golden altar, where he was transformed. Although he was a part of the Ancient One and knew that he was god, his actions were restricted to those of a son. He and the archangel left the golden altar to enter the separated cell.

Some of the evil angels who came in contact with him either covered their hearts or moved out of his path because of the degree of their evilness. On occasion, the archangel removed the angels with hardened hearts from his path.

Ramis learned that another messenger would come who was related in a special way to the Ancient One, but he was still not able to fully understand how it would happen. He felt threatened with losing control of his newly developed kingdom. As Ramis found out about the chosen son, he attempted to murder him, not knowing that he was protected by a seal from the Ancient One.

THE RANSOM

The son communicated to Ramis the message from his father, asking him to release the angels. Although Ramis had no intention of releasing the captives or accepting any ransom, he spitefully replied, "There is no being who belongs to the cell of the Ancient One or to the separated cell who is capable of redeeming the angels." The angels with hardened hearts cheered Ramis on as they mocked and laughed at the son and blasphemed the Ancient One.

In despair, the son immediately returned to the Ancient One to deliver Ramis's message, which became a covenant for the angel's redemption. The son was perplexed by the thought that redemption of the angels was impossible.

As the son presented Ramis's response to the Ancient One, some of the children and angels wept because the angels in the separated cell appeared to be unredeemable. But the faithful continued to praise the Ancient One and offered sacrifices around the bronze altars for the redemption of the fallen angels because they knew that they were unable to comprehend the wisdom of the Ancient One.

The time arrived for the implementation of the redemption plan. The Ancient One communicated the plan to his son and informed all of the angels and children in his cell about his plan to fulfill the covenant for the redemption of the angels.

The god of sanctification, in order to combat evil, had already fallen into the body of an archangel and then into the son of the Ancient One. Now he had to fall farther down the creation chain into the form of an angel. As an angel, his godly powers would be removed, and he would be restricted to the characteristics of an angel.

As he fell into the separated cell, he took on an angel's characteristics, but because he was pure and good, he would not carry the weight of evil upon him. He would, however, become vulnerable to Ramis's temptation.

Like the inhabitants of the separated cell, he received the senses of sight, taste, touch, smell, and hearing because he was separated from the cell of the Ancient One. This had to be done to qualify him to redeem the fallen angels and to fulfill Ramis's covenant that he unwittingly spoke in anger. Ramis covenant that he spitefully uttered limited the being capable of becoming the ransom to the cell of the Ancient One or the separated cell not from both. The god of sanctification would qualify as a being of both cells—a god in the cell of the Ancient One and an angel in the separated cell.

The chosen son appeared in the temple on the golden altars in the midst of the incense. Suddenly, the worshippers around the four bronze altars were able to see him as if he were on the altars in their respective locations throughout the temple. The son became a winged lamb, and he lifted from the altar and flew toward the separated cell below.

As the lamb landed upon the cell, he was converted to the form of an angel and became restricted to the separated cell. The communication between him and the Ancient One was also restricted to that allowed an angel.

In the separated cell, the Ancient One replaced eternity with time to allow for the judgment and destruction of all evil. The chosen angel's imagination became a pathway to allow the rededicated angels and those susceptible to the word of the Ancient One to voluntarily enter through him to begin their journey home.

As soon as the chosen angel landed, he met angels who were waiting and searching for the doctrine. He shared and taught the Ancient One's doctrine and strengthened the angels who chose to undergo the redemption process with food and water from the Ancient One's cell to prepare them for their pilgrimage to their eternal home.

The angels who chose to enter his pathway would continue to be vulnerable to Ramis's temptation and tribulation but would have committed themselves to starve to death the evil within their hearts and replace it with the Ancient One's doctrine as they travelled the pathway.

The angels who were in Ramis's slave camp, where he reinforced his security around them, were allowed by the Ancient One to answer yes in their hearts to accepting his doctrine and to begin the redemption process by proxy through the pathway of the chosen angel.

Ramis and his evil regime knew that a redeemer would come to save the angels, but they did not know who it would be, the time, or the place. He began to search desperately for the chosen angel in order to murder him before he could redeem and purify the angels and disrupt the operation of his kingdom.

He became aware of the pathway in the chosen angel that was used for the redemption process and eventually found a way to enter. He came in contact with angels who had previously served him but had accepted the redemption plan. Therefore, it was easy for him to cause some of them to defile their garments.

Meanwhile, in the temple, the golden altar was prepared in all its splendour, with its sparkling, lit, golden candlesticks in the midst of the living spirits of all creation. All of the murdered angels, children, and soldiers who had died fighting for the Ancient One also waited in part of the golden altar in white robes for the lamb to be sacrificed in order to reinstate those who loved the Ancient One.

Everyone in the chamber of the golden altar focused on the wooden altar adjacent to it. It was complete with its utensils and paraphernalia. The archangels stationed around it were dressed in their ceremonial robes and regalia as they waited to assist with the preparation of the offering of the sacrificial lamb for the ransom of the angels.

Ramis made every attempt to stop the chosen angel from reaching the point where he would become the sacrificial lamb because he knew that the covenant would be fulfilled and that the enslaved angels would be freed against his will.

He never imagined that a deity from the cell of the Ancient One would fall into a creation as an angel in the separated cell to qualify to be slain in order to pay the ransom for his captives. This great love of the Ancient One was unimaginable to Ramis.

After all of the fallen angels had heard the doctrine and decided whether to accept or reject it, the chosen angel appeared on the wooden altar in the temple to be sacrificed as a ransom for the fallen angels.

There was a great silence and sadness in the temple. But immediately after the lamb was sacrificed, the door that connected the cell of the Ancient One to the pathway of the chosen angel's imagination opened, and water and fire flowed from the golden altar, through the door, and into the pathway to purify the angels who were travelling back to their eternal home.

Then the separated cell was grafted onto the cell of the Ancient One, and four archangels were sent from the temple to destroy every evil that existed in the separated cell, including Ramis, his beast, the evil angels, and all other creation.

After the archangels completed their assignment, all activity within the Ancient One's cell came to a standstill as all of creation began singing and praising the Ancient One. There was a great reunion in the cell, and all of the altars in the temple were continuously filled with sacrifices.

Then the god of sanctification, who had lowered himself to redeem the angels, returned to his position as god. And the Ancient One, in his magnificent glory, appeared on his royal throne in his sanctuary, sending and receiving pure light from all of his creation through the golden altar, as it was in the beginning.

The End

NOTES

9 781952 062667